Through the Window

A Journey to the Borderlands of Faerie

Marcie Lynn Tentchoff

Illustrations by Michelle J.A. McIntyre

Other Double-Edged Publishing Titles

Servant of the Manthycore by Michael Ehart
ISBN: 978-0-9793079-5-9
Infinite Realities by R. L. Copple
ISBN: 978-0-9793079-6-6
Seven Archangels: Annihilation by Jane Lebak
ISBN: 978-0-9793079-5-9
Deuces Wild: Beginners' Luck by L. S. King
ISBN: 978-0-9793079-8-0

DEP Anthologies:

Distant Passages, Vol. 1 edited by Bill Snodgrass
ISBN: 978-0-9793079-0-4
Distant Passages, Vol. 2 edited by Selena Thomason
ISBN: 978-0-9793079-1-1
Distant Passages, Vol. 3 edited by Scott Appleton
Coming in 2008!

Marcie Lynn Tentchoff's collection, *Through The Window*, takes readers on a lyrical journey through a hidden world of myth and magic. There be dragons here, creatures Fae and rare, all portrayed with a fresh eye and sense of wonder. The art of Michelle J.A. McIntyre is the perfect addition to Marcie's collection.

-- Jaime Lee Moyer, Poetry Editor, *Ideomancer Speculative Fiction*

When you peek *Through the Window* you glimpse creatures out of legend, beautiful and strange. Michelle McIntyre shows you what to expect in this field guide to some of the denizens of faerie. Marcie Tentchoff's enchanting explanations complement the colorful illustrations very well. Each page-size illustration is accompanied by a poem of approximately 1 page in length. The illustrations seem designed to please small children as well as their parents, but the poems will be too sophisticated for the youngest members of the audience. As for the rest of you, it's time to delve into the lives of dragons, unicorns, and fairies. You are in good hands."

-- David C. Kopaska-Merkel, Editor, *Dreams and Nightmares Magazine*

The poems in *Through the Window* beautifully illuminate the thoughts of the fairy-tale creatures depicted in Michelle McIntyre's jewel-toned illustrations. Here are Parrot Dragons, cursed lovers, Tiger Gryphons, wandering unicorns, petulant centaurs, and even an unexpected encounter between a dragon and a raccoon. I especially enjoyed the fact that most of Marcie Lynn Tentchoff's poems herein employ rhyming verse; she handles sonnet and villanelle with a delicate touch and the result would make an excellent primer for grade-school students learning poetry forms."

-- Samantha Henderson, author of *Heaven's Bones: A Novel of the Mists*

-=-

About the Author

Marcie Lynn Tentchoff has been writing both fantasy and poetry since she was very young. She has degrees in both literature and creative writing, and is an Aurora Award winning poet, with multiple Rhysling nominations. Marcie lives on the west coast of Canada with her family and a number of animals, from the semi-domesticated, a cockatiel, and numerous cats, to the mostly wild, raccoons, deer, bear, and cougar. She refuses to say whether she has ever been to Faerie herself, but she does admit that one can see strange things in the BC woods, when the light is just right.

-=-

About the Artist

Michelle J.A. McIntyre specializes in colored pencil works on fiber-enhanced paper. She creates a variety of fantasy art subject matter including dragons, unicorns, gryphons, fairies, and centaurs, and her work has been featured as magazine covers as well as framed art.

Through the Window
A Journey to the Borderlands of Faerie

Marcie Lynn Tentchoff

Illustrations by Michelle J.A. McIntyre

Double-Edged Publishing
Cordova, Tennessee
www.doubleedgedpublishing.com

Cover and illustrations: Michelle J.A. McIntyre © 2008

ISBN: 978-0-9793079-9-7

Library of Congress Control Number: 2008925722

Double-Edged Publishing, Inc.
9618 Misty Brook Cove
Cordova, Tennessee 38016

www.doubleedgedpublishing.com

For the word of God is living and active. Sharper than any double-edged sword, it penetrates even to dividing soul and spirit, joints and marrow; it judges the thoughts and attitudes of the heart.

Hebrews 4:12 New International Version (NIV)

Printed in the United States of America

First Printing

I dedicate this book to a pair of teachers who have influenced my life and my writing: to June Wilson, who used to tell me that I was "more of a metaphysical poet," and to the memory of Ann Messenger, who I dearly wish had lived to see this book.

- Marcie Lynn Tentchoff

Illustrations inspired by the writers of fantasy who continue to spin such wonderful tales.

- Michelle J.A. McIntyre

Table of Contents

Foreword

Something magical occurs when art meets poetry. A few weeks ago, I had the opportunity to participate in an art gallery poetry reading where poets read a mixture of nature poems, speculative poems, ekphrastic poems and haiku in a tour guide approach. As each poet stood front of paintings which either resonated with or, in some cases, were the inspiration for their poems, I discovered new nuances in each painting that I hadn't noticed on my first viewing. In the background, musicians played baroque-era instruments as the poetry, the art, and the music worked together to weave a spell of enchantment. Reading Marcie Tentchoff's new collection of poetry comes as close as you can to simulating this sort of fantastical experience without physically standing in an art gallery with live musicians.

Lavishly illustrated by Michelle J.A. McIntyre, "Through the Window," will transport you into a realm of tiger gryphons, mermaids, centaurs, faerie folk, and serpents. There is music here, too, in the rhythms and rhymes of formal verse, the refrain of a villanelle, the crescendo of a sonnet, the riff of a triolet, and the rhythm of a cinquain sequence. Even when Tentchoff is not writing in forms, her work is very metrical with a strong sense of rhythm. Her poems sing.

And, what a song!

Tentchoff is known for her speculative poetry and she doesn't disappoint, following the poetic traditions of Homer and Lewis Carroll, as she writes powerfully of mythical beasts and magical realms.

What, you might ask, is speculative poetry? Its simplest definition is "a science fiction, fantasy, or horror poem." I prefer the somewhat vaguer description of "a poem with a fantastical element of some kind." Each poem in this collection opens a new window to a fantastical world, one populated with the creatures of our childhood myths and fantasies. Each song reacquaints us with a world we might have thought we outgrew, but have been secretly missing in our mundane worlds of bills, soccer games, and reality TV.

Somewhere along the way, the stresses and responsibilities of our adult lives can make us close windows to the worlds of our dreams. Tentchoff's poems remind us to leave the windows open a little, so we can hear the songs of faeries and dream of dragons....

-Deborah P Kolodji
President, Science Fiction Poetry Association.

Acknowledgments

I'd like to gratefully acknowledge the support of my family, of my editors, and of the talented and ever-patient poets of Hitting the Muse.

Poems previously appearing elsewhere:

"We'll Not Sail Out on Fridays" - first published in *The Sword Review* May 2005

"Mythic" - first published in *Between Kisses* Dec. 2006

"Hush" - first published in *Vampire Dan's Story Emporium* Winter 2001

"The Dragon's Villanelle" - first published in *Pulp Eternity* 2000

-- Marcie Lynn Tentchoff

Through the Window
A Journey to the Borderlands of Faerie

Marcie Lynn Tentchoff

Illustrations by Michelle J.A. McIntyre

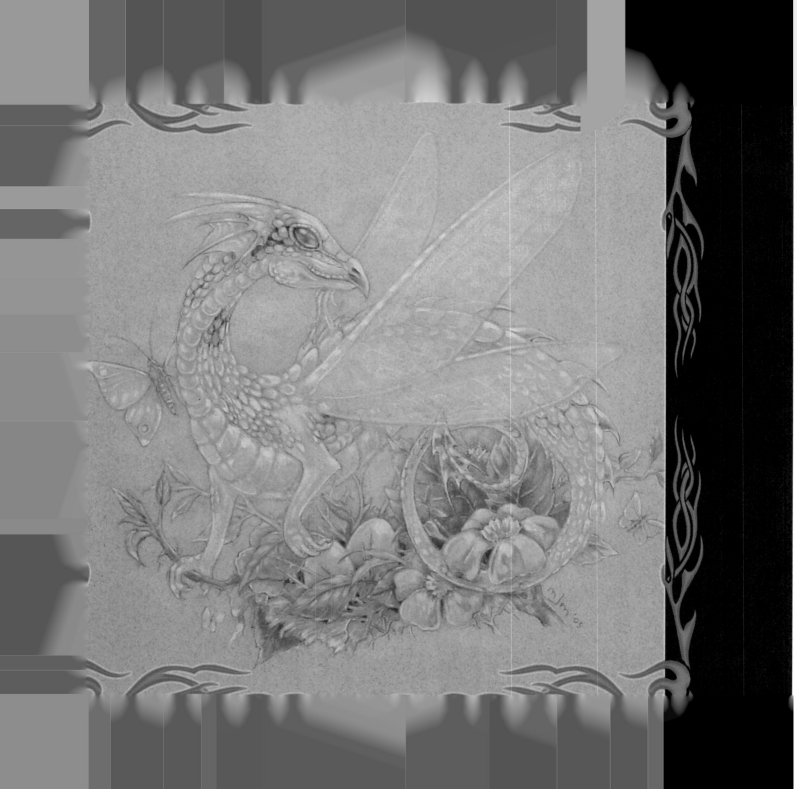

*T*hrough the Window

I long to see the fairy dragons' nest,
to help them gather flowers in the sun,
to sing them softly to their evening rest,
when wingtips still and all their work is done.

I long to join the unicorns that run
and race their shadows over gilded plains,
to count the silk bound dewdrops that are spun
like gemstones through their foam-white tails and manes.

But mortal blood is flowing through my veins,
and youth has bound me to my school and books,
and I, or so I'm told, should not complain,
nor steam the window glass with misty looks.

The borderlands are not so far away
that anyone would notice should I stray.

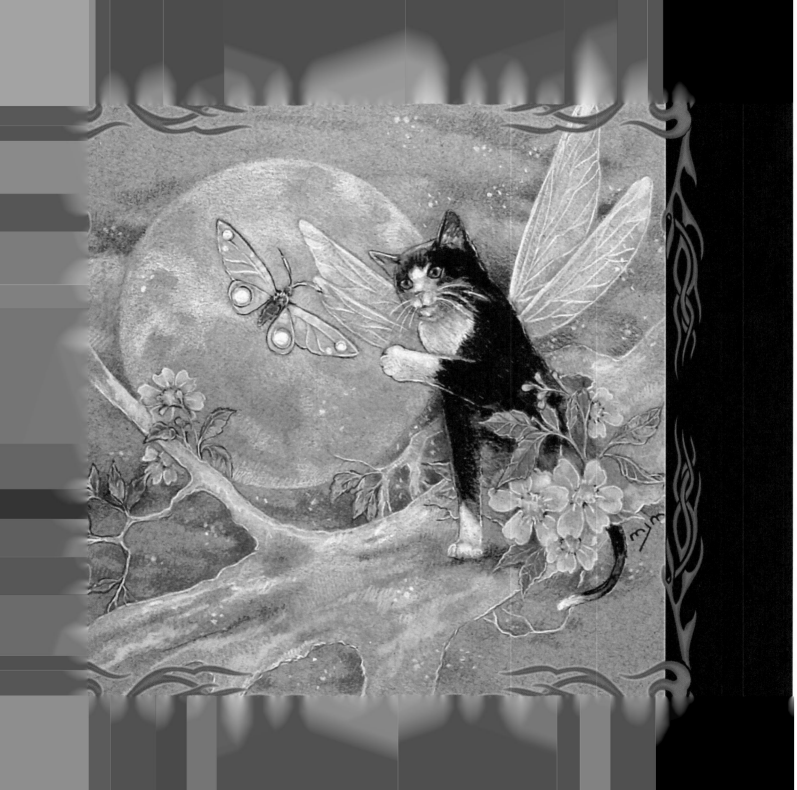

${\mathcal{P}}$rowling

By night
my cousins prowl the ground,
and sing their challenges
in sharp, discordant meowling
to the moon.

They hunt
for tiny rodents, and, in trash cans,
dig for stinking scraps of fish,
and half chewed burgers
for their meals.

They fight
by starlight, claws and canines
tearing swaths of fur that float
adrift in mist-like clouds to
fog the air.

While I,
my gossamer wings spread wide
to catch the midnight breezes,
purr, and tap the bats and fireflies
out of the sky.

One Summer's Day

I saw the fairy queen one day
out sunning in a grassy glade
surrounded by her court of Fae,
her dragon page, her dryad maid....

I saw her smile and dance and play
beside the border, unafraid,
while I watched, not too far away,
well hidden in a building's shade.

A mortal spy, I did not stray,
but tarried lest I be forbade
to watch another such display -
I drank the magics I surveyed,

and kept them, that they might allay
the pointless cruelties that pervade
our mortal lives in great array,
and leave us hopeless and dismayed.

Though time may turn my hair to gray,
though memories and fancies fade,
I saw the fairy queen one day
out sunning in a grassy glade.

Uneasy Boundaries

We do not venture where the wolves are,
where the trees grow close and tall,
past the endpoints of our meadows,
past the mist-wreathed forest wall.

We only linger near the borders,
flowers blooming where we stand,
seeking out their shade-gray bodies,
drifting past our grazing land.

We only watch them as they watch us,
from the corners of our eyes,
guarding our uneasy boundaries,
beast from beast and spy from spy.

We do not seek to break the treaties,
do not yearn to end our peace,
only stand and wait in patience,
for this troubled calm to cease.

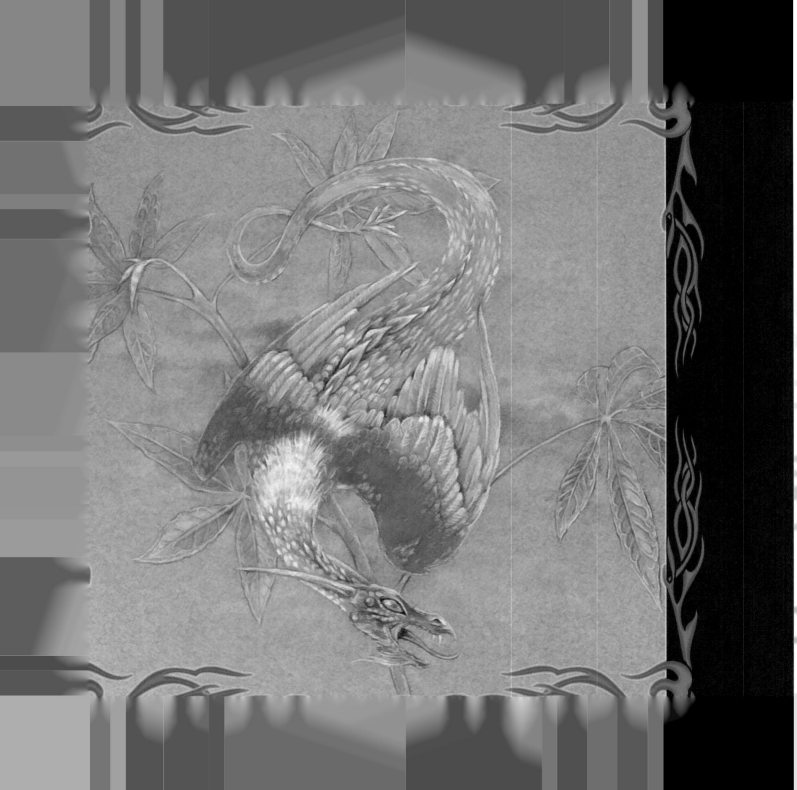

The Parrot Dragon's Chanty

When I first was born one Faerie morn,
and my mother looked at me,
well she shook her head as she sadly said,
"lad, you're bound for ship and sea.
With your plumage bright you look such a fright,
other dragons will all mock."
So she packed me down to a seaside town
and she left me on the dock.

With a "Yo Heave Ho" I was sad to go,
but I knew me mum was right,
so I sought the back of a tarry Jack
and we sailed that very night.

With a shoulder view I joined the crew
and we traveled near and far,
and I never railed against setting sail,
or complained of salt or tar.
Well the work is rough and the vittles tough,
but the sights that I have seen,
make me glad indeed of the life I lead
and the places I have been.

With a "Yo Heave Ho" when the Fae winds blow
and our ship is running free,
I'd never trade one shipmate's braid
for a life without the sea.

We'll Not Sail Out on Fridays

Once....

Sailing ships skimmed over seas
where serpents lurked and sirens sang,
and every sailor worth his pay
knew pea soup summoned up a storm,

while Friday sailings brought foul luck,
and cans, miss-opened, even more,
and all the souls of sailors dead
turned into gulls to call them home.

Now....

Airplanes speed by overhead
and oil slicks begrime the waves
where dolphins romped and mermaids combed
out strands of kelp-dark, flowing hair,

and every landsman knows that truth
is only found in scholars' books,
while any beast that lurks below
can be seen, stuffed, in some museum.

But....

We still hear voices in the wind
and let the seagulls eat their fill,
and we'll not sail out on Fridays,
nor open cans save right side up.

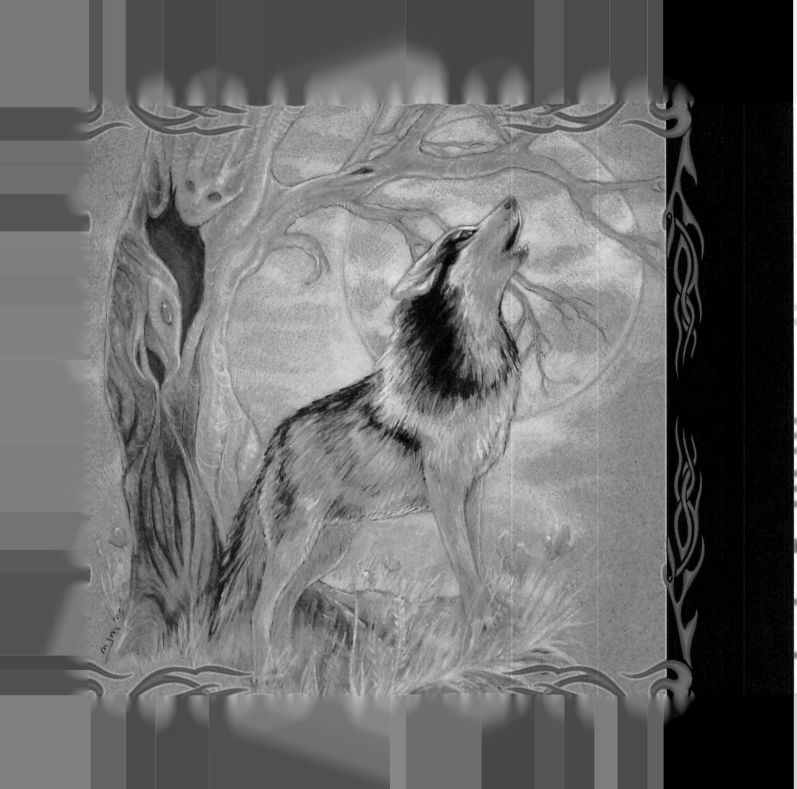

Cursed

"Love conquers all."
That's what I said to her,
and walked up to the border's edge
to take her hand.

I smiled and coaxed,
and bid her come to me,
to join my wild, enchanted life
beneath the stars.

Love conquers all...
That's what I thought before
my parents found that we had wed
and cast their spell.

"No more of this,"
my mother whispered as
she changed my form, and trapped my wife
within a tree.

"Love conquers all,
and ours will keep you safe
from any little mortal tramp
who seeks your hand."

They think they've won.
They think I'll roam away
in wolven form, and leave her here
to root behind.

But they are wrong,
and though they've magiked us
to live two lonely, separate lives...
Love conquers all.

Moon Dance

The full moon rides the sky tonight
as pale and chill as frosted glass.
It bathes the tree tops in its light

while we below dance through the grass,
and breathe the midnight magics in,
enchantment in each circling pass.

It's now that all bright dreams begin,
when wishes clamor to be made,
when spells and charms all sing and spin,

and spiral through our misty glade.
But should we catch them as they fly,
all dreams and wishes slowly fade,

and so we let them pass us by,
to weave their mad and magic tune,
in otherwheres beyond our sky,

while we, abandoned, do not cry,
but dance beneath the Autumn moon.

$\mathcal{B}$lood Red

Blood Red, they call me,
scarlet minded, scarlet marked,
for times of battle.

It's thus they raised me,
training me to match the color
of my crimson scales.

I learned my lessons,
know the twenty seven levels
of consuming flame,

the use of jaw and claw
and razor wing to rend and spill the
substance of my name.

And yet, in slumber,
sometimes pale dreams find me,
pastel-hued, and clinging,

offering a hazy picture
of some other, gentler life,
where no blood flows.

Herd Mentality

I won't go back to join my herd,
to let them tease and call me names,
or pull my hair and tweak my tail...
I'm far too old for childish games.

We centaur folk, so legends say,
are brave and stern and grim and wise,
so why must all my herdmates joy
in turning legends into lies?

Perhaps apart they might behave,
might read thick books or gaze at stars,
but in a group they much prefer
fake martial arts to watching Mars.

It's just not right or good or fair,
and so, that's that, I give my word --
unless I'm "it" next time we play
I won't go back to join my herd.

Strange Siblings

Our mother raised us both
within her leafy nest.
She cleaned your scales as
lovingly, as sweetly
as she did my fur.

And when your wings unfurled,
I know she taught you
of the joys of flight
as best she could,
and sought out help

from mocking birds and jays,
that you might learn
far more than she,
an earth-bound maid,
could hope to know.

Me she taught of other things,
the leaf mould smell
of autumn days, and how
to hide amid the grass
by standing still.

And when we left her,
you to seek the ways of air,
and sunlit days,
and draughts of nectar
served by fairy hand,

and I to run along the ground,
and steal sweet nuts,
and sweeter cheese
from hazel groves
and farmers' wives,

she stood alone, just swaying
softly in the rising breeze,
and watched us go,
as siblings always,
foster children of a tree

At Twilight

When twilight paints the sky with pink and blue,
and drains far tree tops to a mist-pale hue,
when even hopes and joys have bleached to grey
and turned somehow to trials for us to rue,

It's time to turn our backs upon the day,
hold frenzied thoughts and worries all at bay
close weary eyes on tasks left yet undone
and let our waking burdens slip away.

On both sides of the border nets are spun,
with faerie folk and human caught as one
in days that put our strengths to bitter test,
and make us doubt the projects we've begun.

If endless daytimes lead to lives obscessed,
then let us seek out bed or den or nest,
where all our pressing goals are set askew,
and gentle dreaming heals us as we rest.

Dangerous Games

We've had our fill of empty pleasures,
drinking dewdrops, tending blooms,
flying free above the meadows,
singing sweetly in the dells.

Too young we are, and full of fire,
to meekly gather spider silk.
There is something more, we know it,
than this dreary, proper life.

And so we seek out bright adventures,
daring fancies, dangerous games,
risk and madness, free and flowing -
there is nothing half so sweet.

To creep up close behind the serpent,
touch his skin and tweak his tail,
then hide among the flower petals
till he passes safely by.

Or steal the merfolk's salt sea treasure,
from their cave above the tide,
and mocking, leave a trail of baubles
leading up into the trees.

Or taunt the fire bird as he's flying,
dancing just outside his reach,
or steal a mortal maiden's lover,
laughing sweetly as she weeps.

The Freedom of the Skies

To mount between a dragon's wings
and rise into the open sky,
to know the joy that soaring brings
when clouds themselves are not too high,
and mountain peaks go speeding by
like wavelets on a misty sea.
I'd gladly bid the ground goodbye
if only you would set me free.

To serve enchanted queens and kings
beyond the faerie borders I
might ride in quest of mystic rings,
with shadow-armored wizards vie --
their evil wishes I'd defy,
then with their treasures I would flee,
to leave them plotting, foul and sly,
if only you would set me free.

I long to search out magic things,
to catch some handsome prince's eye,
but something deep inside me clings
to earthbound life, all pale and shy,
and leaves me here, alone, to cry
in my own room, where none can see.
I'd leave this place without a sigh
if only you would set me free.

Oh Fear, I'd mount, and ride, and fly,
and be the hero I should be,
if only second thoughts would die,
if only you would set me free.

Mythic

I won't believe in unicorns,
all purity, and wild joy,
who revel in reflecting pools
and flowers blooming in the snow,
or dragons with their jewel-etched wings,
who ride the winds in search of gold
to catch the sparks from deep red gems
and stoke the fires of their hoards,
or dryads wreathed in leafy hair,
or sirens with their haunting song,
or elf-folk dancing on the grass,
or fairies in their petal beds.
I wont believe in Summer days,
with gentle warmth to dull my pain,
or icicles that scatter rays
of rainbow light upon the clouds,
or anything outside this room,
this prison formed of rules and truth,
where hope is such a bitter word...
I won't believe, I *can't* believe.

Grounded

I used to leave my bed and fly
upon a white-winged zebra's back—
we'd race the breezes in the sky.
I used to leave my bed and fly
but now I lie awake and cry,
and curse the dreams that I now lack—
I used to leave my bed and fly
upon a white-winged zebra's back

$\mathcal{P}$rotector

I wake to the sound of wing beats,
to tiny gusts of wind that
tangle up my greying hair
and set the scent of years long past
to fill my nose and tease my mind.

You stand beside me, waiting ,
larger now than once you were
when first your mother,
dying from a human's lance thrust,
sealed me to your care and training....

but only just. Dragons, it seems,
are slow to grow, while I,
a mortal man for all my skills,
now hobble with my jewel-topped staff
to fix your morning meal.

We travel onward,
me before you, standing tall
to shield you from the enemies
your mother said would
surely come to seek you out.

And yet these days my footsteps falter,
and I fear that someday soon,
I will not wake to feed you,
for this road is long and weary,
and I, being old, more weary still.

Hush

Do not cry my little dragon
Mama's here to dry your eyes
Papa's hunting trolls for dinner
Home is warm and safe and dry.
I will bring you jewels tomorrow.
You can add them to your hoard.
Do not fear they'll be discovered,
No one knows where they are stored.
Someday you will have a maiden,
Tasty morsels, sweet and soft,
You will make her mount upon you,
Spread your wings and leap aloft.
Someday you will meet a dragon,
Fair and wise and just like me,
Court and love and rise a'mating,
And a grandame I will be.
So close your eyes my little spark-ling,
Hush your cries and go to sleep.
Do not fear the evil humans,
Mama will a Knightwatch keep.

*B*elow the Surface

Water-witch, you know I hear you
singing in your misty pool.
Your voice is sweet,
and low and calm
as water on a windless day.

You tempt me so to venture near,
beckoning with every note,
each haunting phrase,
each murmured hint
of life below the water line.

But I am far too wise to stand,
lingering at your pond's cool edge.
I've heard the tales,
and dried the tears
of those who heeded your dark songs.

But, Water-witch, although I go,
leaving you to sing alone,
in honesty
I wish I might
just one time glimpse your shimmering world.

$\mathcal{T}$he Dragon's Villanelle

The wonders and the glories of my cave,
The caverns deep which few men ever know,
Are viewed not by the wise but by the brave.

Each golden chamber silent as the grave,
Where sapphire streams, and emerald ceaseless flow,
The wonders and the glories of my cave.

One human corpse within my hoard I save,
And there, the gems which once made him my foe
Are viewed not by the wise but by the brave.

He stood outside my door to rant and rave,
Demanding, lance held firm, that I forego
The wonders and the glories of my cave.

Now in my mind that hero's but a knave.
And thus, my claim that all the sights below
Are viewed not by the wise but by the brave.

Go home and dream the magics that you crave.
Be glad that you still live to be let go.
The wonders and the glories of my cave
Are viewed not by the wise but by the brave.

The Thief

I set out traps to catch a bandit bold,
so skilled a thief he'd filched a sparkling jewel
from deep within my stack of hoarded gold.
The other dragons think that I'm a fool,
to bother making traps to simply hold,
when flaming rogues can scarce be seen as cruel.
But I think if I set this rascal free,
he might be swayed to gather gems for me.

The Tiger Gryphon Tempted

I don't know why he follows me --
he's always just a pace behind,
his night black wings bewitch my mind
and leach away my clarity.

I'm told crows follow where wolves run,
to feast upon the hunters' kills,
and once, I'll own, I had such skills,
to stalk and rend... Those days are done.

For I have turned from blood-filled ways,
denied both hawk and cat free reign,
and though it goes against the grain,
I'll hunt no more through all my days.

A beast I am, but old and proud,
long eons past my rash-lived youth,
and yet, he hints at older truth,
at feasts my oaths have not allowed.

And deep within my heart I know,
he tests me with his company
and makes me doubt my policy--
Temptation clothed as carrion crow.

Coiled

I wait,
horned head held low.
My wingtips barely stir.
The grass and leaves feel cool against
my scales.

So still,
while butterflies
land trembling on my coils,
tasting them for nectar just like
flowers.

Time drags.
The sun dips low
and shadows slowly fall,
while I lurk, hungry, in my nest
and wait.

Rhymer

"Violets for faithfulness,"
that's what you tell me when
you leave me here, sheltered by
blue-purple blooms.

And I believe you, mostly,
gazing at the snaking border
where it twists its way between
your lands and mine.

You'll come again, that much
is surely true. You can't seem
to resist my world's endless magic,
or its siren call.

You cross, you shrink to violet size,
we touch, and talk of tales I've heard,
of folk and places I have seen...
and then you leave.

You speak of love each time we meet,
and do not lie, for I have seen you glowing
as you scribble down the words I say
upon your page.

And yet, for all your constancy and
love-lit eyes, I do not think it's me you want,
when you sit, smiling in the violets,
stealing poems between each kiss.

$\mathcal{I}$mpossible

We seldom listen to crows.
They talk...and talk and talk
and talk, and talk...
incessantly, sardonically,
but little that they say makes sense.

Almost, perhaps, I might believe
their too-snide squawks
of "shop - ping malls,"
great caverns where
young mortal people spend their days.

Or of the hives of mirrored glass
that mortal folk have mounded up
in place of trees, and grass,
and sprigs and sprouts,
and all the beauty that we love.

But when the crows caw of the way
most mortals talk ...
and talk and talk, and talk and talk,
incessantly, sardonically,
to scraps of metal in their hands...

...I think again.

Changes

By Sylphen's Wood I gather flowers,
hearing whispers of his name
in among the leaf-draped bowers
where last summer we both came
to meet and while away the hours,
talking, laughing, holding hands,
and dancing where the Dream Oak towers
at the edge of mortal lands.
But summer sunshine turns to showers,
time moves on as leaves turn gold,
and love itself from sweetness sours,
changing seasons, bitter cold.

Scales

Men do not praise my singing
as they do the nightingale's,
nor value it against the trillings
of the crested lark.

Those songbirds catch the sounds
of forests in their gentle calls,
their dreams of water flowing
in their gurgled notes.

They sooth, caress, and comfort Men,
reminding them of fragile things,
like peace, and calm, and growing trees,
which Men can change.

While I? I sing of treasures buried
in some lonely cave, where creatures
greater far than I curl sleeping
round a hoard of gold.

Of maidens offered up as bait,
and knights in armor come to joust,
who end at last, their battles done,
my cousins' meals.

Men do not wish reminding
of the musings of the dragon race,
nor of powers we control,
indifferent to the will of Man.

And yet, it does them good, I think,
to hear my soaring, scale-edged song,
discordant to their human ears,
and grating on their human pride.

Heart of Ice

When snowflakes fall he comes for me,
that ghost-pale shape I scarcely see
against the diamond patterned frost --
white in the wind his mane is tossed,
uncut, and flowing, silken free.

He stands beneath an ice-glazed tree,
and taps my window mournfully --
his night-black eyes made sad and lost
when snowflakes fall.

But I? I will not heed his plea,
I've left that realm, destroyed its key,
and never more will pay its cost --
let others see that border crossed,
and lose their hearts to pay his fee
when snowflakes fall.

Summer's End

I find you in the meadow
where the wild roses grow,
close beside the singing waters
of an ever flowing stream.
You dance upon the breezes
with your fragile, patterned wings,
as I watch and hide my worries
in my wonder at your grace.

What chrysalis first spawned you?
serpent sleek and dragon proud,
scarcely larger than the blossoms
that dance with you as you pass.
What egg did you first hatch from,
and what creature called you child,
long before I ever met you,
long before I named you friend?

The Summer days are passing,
Autumn nights are closing in,
all the butterflies are waiting
for the call to fly away.
Will Southern warmlands beckon?
Will you leave and not return?
Will you never more lap nectar
from my gently upturned palm?

Storm Casting

two sibling rivals,
mother's favorite, father's choice,
they meet above us
nursing long remembered slights -
storm clouds gather as they chat

whose coils were brightest?
who crushed rocks to finer sand
in his gleaming teeth?
words turn to tangled sparring
lightning crackles through the sky

they tear the heavens,
shatter peaceful silence with
their thuderous roars
their metal scales, in clashing,
scatter spikes of silver sparks

these two storm casters,
serpent bodies twined in hate
as if in friendship,
each striving to be greater,
each afraid that he is less.

By Starlight

When sunlight has departed from the land,
and starshine dots the sky above our heads,
when moonbeams tangle branches in their strands,
and daytime folk are tucked up in their beds,

I walk between the shadow-twisted trees,
my hooves tread lightly just above the ground,
my tail a stream of darkness in the breeze,
my passage reft of tracks, of spoor, of sound...

But where I've been folk toss and turn in sleep,
their inner selves flung wide as I ghost by,
and even while they lie in slumber deep,
bright dreams and dark take shape behind their eyes.

Perhaps I too might see my dreams take flight,
were I not bound to wander through the night.

When the Beast Comes

When the beast comes
we hide among the spreading trees,
scarce moving as we watch and wait,
our hair and wings transforming
into autumn leaves to mask our shape
and grant us safety in the woods.

And when it leaves,
its heaving flanks and swirling fur
turned rank with hot, frustrated sweat,
we laugh, and feast, and tell brave tales
of heroes who out-thought the beast
and taught us tricks to fool its eye.

Yet, in the darkness,
tucked in beds of warmest moss,
our dreams fill with ancestral scenes
of blood red fangs, and night black claws,
and when we wake, we try to mask
uncertainties, like fairies in a nut brown tree.

On My Rock

From on my rock,
I see the surface of
the rippling ocean, stretched,
an endless blue-green jewel,
to meet the sky.

This is my realm,
a land of dream-bright waves,
and darting gem-tone fish,
of underwater palaces,
and cool, dark caves.

Here I have swum
through woods and jungles grown
of waving emerald kelp,
and danced along the coral reefs
to selkie song.

I've been well-loved
by mermaid princesses
who edge my scales with pearls,
well-hated by the sailor lads
I sometimes tease.

And yet, although
I love my salt-sea home
beneath the white-tipped swells,
sometimes I sit upon my rock
and flex my wings.

Such tiny stubs,
compared to those I see
on dragons of the sky.
Almost I wish... but no, such thoughts
are fleeting things.

This is my rock.
Around it flows my world.
Although the air is sweet,
so too's the sea, and when it calls
I'll dive... and fly.

Parting

I hold you in my lap,
stroking tiny golden scales
with fingertips soaked slick
by tears.

I close my eyes and feel
my way along your back,
touching every ridge along
your spine.

I memorize the coils
of your whip thin tail,
the fragile structure of
your face.

Someday, when I am old
enough to take my place
among the ladies of the
faery court,

then you'll be mine, forever
at my side, my dragon page,
companion then as you
are now.

I'll go to school and learn
about our world, and all
that I must know to serve
our queen.

And you'll learn too, in woods
and dusty caves, the things
that growing dragons learn
of life.

But years must pass before
we meet again, and time
can change both future plans
and hearts.

And so I cling to you,
and to my memories
of summer, golden scales,
and love.

$\mathcal{A}$ Roving

There's a road that winds before me
passing lands I do not know --
all it's gentle curves implore me,
and it's clear that I must go

tread the pathways mist-enshrouded,
up tall hills and over plains,
through dim valleys ever-clouded,
by a violet haze of rain,

Seeing fae and untamed creatures,
as I pass along my way,
praying I'll recall their features,
if we meet again someday.

There's an inn off in the distance,
glowing with a friendly light
and it lowers my resistance,
makes me long to rest the night....

But for me there is no stalling,
I can't pause what I've begun,
for the endless road is calling
and my journey's not yet done.

A Note About Traditional Forms Used in this Collection

Part of the fun of writing this book was having the chance to use many different poetic forms, both traditional and modern. Many of the poems were written in free verse, blank verse, and in various simple rhyming patterns, but listed below are a few of the more interesting traditional forms I explored in these pages.

Villanelle – The Dragon's Villanelle
Terza Rima – Moon Dance
Triolet – Grounded
Linked Tankas – Storm Casting
Rondeau – Heart of Ice
Spenserian Sonnet – Through the Window
Linked Cinquains – Coiled
Ottava Rima – The Thief
Ballade – The Freedom of the Skies
Rubáiyát – At Twilight
Shakespearean Sonnet – By Starlight

- Marcie Lynn Tentchoff

Printed in the United States
127931LV00002B

9780979307997